W9-APT-466

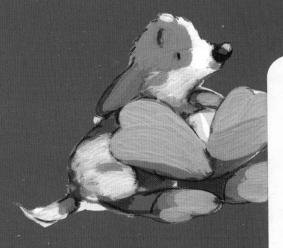

Para Amparo
G. G.

Thank you, Maya!
R. A.

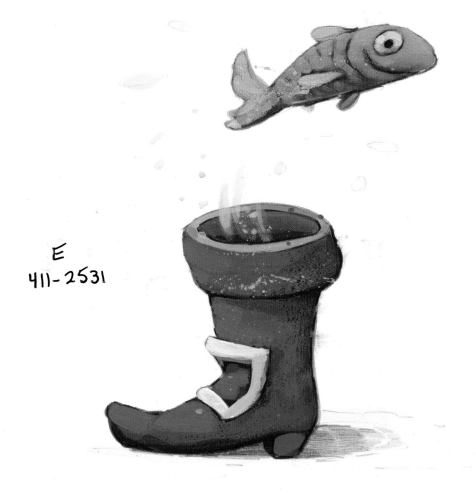

Text copyright © Greg Gormley 2011
Illustration copyright © Roberta Angaramo 2011
First published in Great Britain in 2011 by Gullane Children's Books, 185 Fleet Street, London EC4A 2HS
First published in the United States by HOLIDAY HOUSE, INC. in 2011.
All Rights Reserved
HOLIDAY HOUSE is registered in the U.S. Patent and Trademark Office.
Printed and Bound in February 2012 at Shenzhen Fuweizhi Printing Ltd.,
Longhua Town, Baoan District, Shenzhen, China.
www.holidayhouse.com
First American Edition
3 5 7 9 10 8 6 4

Library of Congress Cataloging-in-Publication Data
Gormley, Greg.
Dog in boots / by Greg Gormley ; illustrated by Roberta Angaramo. — 1st American ed.
p. cm.
ISBN 978-0-8234-2347-7 (hardcover)
[1. Shoes—Fiction. 2. Dogs—Fiction.] I. Angaramo, Roberta, ill. II. Title.
PZ7.G6697Do 2011
[E]—dc22
2010029889

Dog in Boots

by Greg Gormley • illustrated by Roberta Angaramo

Holiday House / New York

Dog was reading a brilliant book, all about a cat
who wore a pair of truly magnificent boots.

When he finished reading, Dog put down his book
and thought a little bit.

Then he went to the local shoe shop.

"Have you got any footwear as splendid as this?"
he asked, showing the book to the shopkeeper.
"I believe I have," said the shopkeeper, and brought out four
just-as-splendid boots, one for each of Dog's paws.
"Bow **WOW!**" said Dog. "I'll take them."

Dog was so pleased that he went straight home . . .

to dig up his very best bone.

But the new boots were not at all splendid or magnificent for digging.
And they got so muddy that they looked quite awful.

So Dog took them back to the shop.

"Have you got some that are better for digging?" he asked.
"I have just the thing," said the shopkeeper.
"These **rain boots** are perfect in mud—
it simply washes right off."

The rain boots were wonderful for digging . . .

but when Dog went for a swim in the pond, they **filled up with water** and he sank with a

PLOP!

Dog took them back to the shop.

"Have you got some that are better for swimming?" he asked.
"The best thing for swimming," the shopkeeper said, "are
flippers."

The flippers were fantastic

for swimming . . .

but when Dog tried to scratch,

they **flip-flap-flopped** around his head

in a very unsatisfying way.

Dog took them back to the shop.

"Have you got some that are better for scratching?" he said.

"I'm glad you asked," said the shopkeeper. "With these **high heels** you can scratch—and look rather fashionable at the same time."

For scratching behind Dog's ears,
the high heels were simply divine. . . .

Unfortunately, they were dreadful to run in—
he went flying head over high heels!

Dog took them back to the shop.

"Have you got some that go a bit faster?" he asked.

"Oh, yes," said the shopkeeper. "If you want to go super-fast, try skis. They go very fast indeed—"

"I'll take them!" said Dog.

And he was gone before the shopkeeper could say,

"—but only on snow!"

Without any snow, Dog's skis didn't move at all.

He couldn't run

or scratch

or swim

or dig.

On his way back to the shop, Dog thought some more. . . .

"Okay," he said to the shopkeeper. "I want something that's good
for digging and swimming and scratching and running.
Oh, nice and furry too. Do you have anything like that?"

"No," said the shopkeeper, "but YOU do.
They're called . . .

PAWS!"

"Perfect!" said Dog.

Dog was so pleased with his nice, furry, practical paws
that he scratched all the fleas from his coat . . .

ran after his tail . . .

swam around and around the queen's lake
until she told him to hightail it out of there . . .

and dug a big hole to rebury his very best bone.

Finally Dog went home and
picked out another brilliant book to read.

This time it was about a girl
who didn't wear any silly boots, but did wear . . .

a lovely red hood!

"Hmmm . . . ," thought Dog.

Little
Red
Riding
Hood